What is Unspoken

38 Musings From

a Grandma,

Real Estate Agent,

and Princeton Grad

Emily Lewis Penn

What is Unspoken

**38 Musings From a Grandma,
Real Estate Agent, and Princeton Grad**

Emily Lewis Penn

New York, New York
Illustrations, Cover Design, and Layout by Catherine Labarca
Book Edited by Shriya Sekhsaria

What is Unspoken

Copyright 2023 © by Emily Lewis Penn

Published by Park Avenue Books

www.Emilyspoetry.com
emilylppoetry@gmail.com

ISBN: 9798393264437

For

Thomas (Tom) Lux, a wonderful poet and and my MFA thesis advisor, whose voice I still hear

Billy Collins, my first MFA workshop teacher, who taught me to look around

Michael Balick, my best friend, husband and cheerleader extraordinaire

Jackie, Miles and Margot, who continue to inspire me, and have taught me to be a mom

Max and Asher, who are teaching me to be a grandmother

Alexander, Beth, Stephen, Dan, Tammy and Boris, who teach me that love grows where love goes

Anna Lewis, my brave and courageous sister, whose compassion changes lives

Bob Roth, who has beautifully read several of the poems herein, on TM's online global group meditations over the last few years

Alisa Matlovsky and Jung Min Lee, who have inspired me with our "6 minute" Princeton Women's Network group

.

The Last Day of 2020

With 2020 vision, Dear Reader, as I sit
at my kitchen table this morning,
coffee in my cup, books piled up to read,
I want to tell you something
important, really important.
I want to tell you lessons I learned
from this year's ups and downs,
this year when such ordinary things
felt, frankly, extraordinary –
things like hugging, shopping, eating
at a diner, flying to see my kids.
I want to tell you these things,
but you and I know
that you have your own lessons.
You don't need mine.
Instead, I toast the bread,
add a pat of butter, pour
myself a third cup of coffee
and wish for you many
blessings in 2021 and beyond.

Contents

Comfort   39

Questions

Morning Meditation

How you see the world
with your eyes closed softly
is how the world shows up
with your eyes wide open.

Each day the sky changes
its color, its hue, its intensity –
My eyes take it in and see
how the sun shows
up on parts of the trees,
and sometimes, not at all.

What am I looking for,
as I look out these windows?
What does this changing light,
this changing wind, this bird
that just flew across
my piece of sky
want to say to me?

The real question is –
What do I want to be asked?

What Does It Mean?

What does it mean to be me?
What does it mean to be you?

What does it mean to learn from mistakes?
What does it mean to try harder?

What does it mean to just be?
What does it mean to live and let live?

What does it mean to love your neighbor?
What does it mean to let bygones be bygones?

What does it mean to Thank God?
What does it mean to make sense of it all?

What does it mean to find your true calling?
What does it mean to fall in love?

What does it mean to forgive and forget?
What does it mean to honor and never forget?

What does it mean to begin again?
What does it mean to be a beginner?

What does it mean to be a friend?
What does it mean to give and receive?

What does it mean to tell the truth?
What does it mean to be kind?

What does it mean to tell your story?
What does it mean, anything is possible?

What If

What if I had studied computer science,
  as my ex-husband exhorted?
What if I had attended the wedding
  in Colombia?
What if I had gone to Spain, instead
  of France, to be an au pair?
What if I had gone to Harvard instead
  of Princeton?
What if I had really learned to swim,
  or ski, or ride a bike, or cook,
  or accept that job?
What if I had been a better mother,
  sister, daughter, wife, friend, person?

What if I had asked more questions,
  better questions?
What if I knew what I mean by better?

What if I had let go of the useless past
  sooner, the past I clung to
  like a broken string of pearls
  stuck in a sock drawer?

What if I had learned to forgive sooner?
What if I had learned to just let go, sooner?

What if I don't go down this rabbit hole,
  and just live?

The Questions I Ask Myself
When I Think No One is Looking

When I wake up in the morning, and I'm the only one
awake, I often ask myself, "How am I?
Am I tired, am I happy, am I excited?"

On this morning, I ask the air –
"Who am I?"

Am I the four-year-old who wails
to Dr. Gilner in the middle of the night,
as he leaves with Stevie, my baby brother,
"Please bring him back"?

Am I the six-year-old who buys the five
cent pack of seeds and dreams of
them growing into pink zinnia cupcakes?

Am I the adolescent who goes to my concrete
backyard with a metal folding chair
to read the "Happy Hollisters", hoping
this book will make me happy?

Am I the young woman giving birth
for the first time, in more pain
than I've ever known on this earth,
and totally present, totally alive?

I don't remember – so much –
I don't remember how things tasted –

The meatballs that Jennifer's grandma made.
I know I loved them.

But how did they taste?
Am I the me who tasted them?

What I do know –
I know I'm not you.
I know that this body did not exist then,
as the cells keep changing.

Something doesn't change.
Something doesn't, change.
Something, doesn't change.
I am that part that doesn't change.

Does This Poem Make Me Look Fat?

> *What makes the engine go?*
> *Desire, desire, desire.*
> *- Stanley Kunitz*

Finish what's on your plate, child.
People in China (Africa, Zimbawe, Bhutan...) are dying of hunger.

Half of humanity lives on less
Than $10 a day; children go to bed hungry.

Chew slowly.
Eat this, not that.

Don't worry, no one ever went to college
With a pacifier in his mouth.

After she announced that she wanted to work at McDonald's,
Her brother said, *That's not something you aspire to,*
It's what you do when you can't do anything else.
But, she replied, *I'd get all the French fries I could eat.*

Did you ever notice that every French movie
Shows people eating?

On your coffee table, the magazine covers promise
Seven foods that will make you thin,
Five foods to show your love handles the door,
Six foods to live longer.

If, like me, you have more books on how to lose weight
Than how to understand astronomy, entomology

Or even archeology, consider this.

When did eating become the enemy?

The more we obsess, the fatter we get.
You get what you fear, don't you?

Absence

And Then You Are Gone

This morning I sit at the kitchen table,
as is my custom, and look again, outside,
and watch you, Dear Bird, as you swoop
down tentatively until you enter
the birdhouse this cold December day.

You feast with abandon until I look up
from my papers, startled, by the sounds
of your flapping wings.
And then you are gone.

Should I focus now on this brief time
we spent together – though apart?
You held my attention for a short while.
Or on the emptiness I feel of your absence,
your uncanny ability to live,
or so it seems, to my untrained eyes,
in only the here,
and only the now?

Uncle Deane, A Life Well Lived

A day, such as today
doesn't make sense.
True, it is cold and March 6th.
There is a slight breeze,
the sun is shining, brightly,
unaware that everywhere
you look, there's a lack,
of a man no longer here,
doing what he did –
laughing at your jokes,
listening when you talked,
being there, everywhere,
when you played soccer,
lacrosse, volleyball, when
you danced and danced
and danced, when
you graduated from kindergarten,
middle school, college,
medical school, got married.
What he might say, were
he here to say it –
Remember my smile.
Hold my love in your heart.
Do what you can today
for yourself, for everyone
you love, no one is perfect,
be patient with yourself
first, be patient with
the world, the world
needs your love.

Anxiety of Seven O'Clock

I wake with the dread
of things undone, dead
days gone by -
I look out the window
and don't feel the joy
of morning, just the
sadness of mourning
again, and the weight
of - being late -
in this early light.

Runaway Hat

Showing off, when I first owned you,
    I showed you off, and pulled you out
    of the bag. You fell
    into the grimy street that dark and snowy night.

Later at the theater, you were almost
    left under the seat after the show.
And now –

You are gone,
    left in the subways of New York City,
    ready to be on your own,
    out of your comfort zone,
    where you warmed my head
    so stylishly.

My sweet, unprotected wanderer,
    you are lost, but not forgotten.

You are a precious thing, like a word
    is a thing, possibly forgotten if not
    written down.

I send you my love, Little Hat, and hope
     that whoever finds you wears you
    in good health and cold weather,
    proudly,
    and treats you well.

The End of November 2020

Winter is almost here
my Darling, though the calendar
says it has already arrived.

For me, the beginning of December
marks the real onset of winter
with its holiday lights and sparkle,
giving and receiving,
and yet – how I will miss
the beauty of Autumn,
and how – for me – Autumn marks,
as it has since I was a child,
the beginning of beginnings –
a new school year,
new notebooks,
new backpacks,
new clothing,
a fresh beginning.

But now, this late
November morning,
I worry about the people
in my own United States,
who don't have enough to eat,
the old people, the parents,
the children.

I worry that worry isn't enough.
Worry will not feed
the empty stomachs.

The Luxury of Many Problems

The washing machine stopped washing.
I got a cold yesterday.
The babysitter didn't show up.

Oh, how lovely to have problems.
That I can whine to God, the universe
and to you, my best friend,
in the mirror, feels good,
in an odd way.
Comforting.

It means, don't you think,
that none of my problems
are bigger
than all these,
when you can think
of nothing else,
like, for my friend,
whose daughter died
last week in a bathtub
from a seizure,
or my other friend,
who is dealing
with stage four cancer
or the six-year-old
in Ukraine who
lost his mom and dad
to war,
and can't think of any
of his other problems?

Unleavened Bread

*(Kaddish for the 1.5 million babies and
children who perished in the Sho'ah)*

Close your eyes, don't think
of Macha in Stutthof, how cold
the night was and how, to keep warm, she slipped
her hands under her dead neighbor's armpits. Don't
think about the Lodz camp for children --
you might see Teresa Jabubowska,
dead at age ten from 100 blows
she received for the bread she stole,
or of Yitskhok who traded his shoes for two
pieces of bread before he died.
Did you know that the Nazis killed pregnant women,
and if they delivered, killed their babies?
Don't look at the newborn, nose pinched shut
by another tortured Jew, so the Nazis would think it stillborn
and spare its mother from certain death.
 Close your ears to Eva,
whose mamamamamama
pierced the frozen air, after five days in a sealed boxcar,
her mother's breasts empty of milk.
They both licked the air to wet their lips,
her mother's tongue so dry she couldn't speak
as they entered the oven.
Don't think of "Cat in Boot's" who knocked
out Tamarah's teeth and eyes, and hung
her on a rack. If you do you might think this
happened, might be afraid, worry

this could happen again, and how could it?

Silence these memories in your cells,

so we may all live in peace.

What is Unspoken

Amelia rings the doorbell Tuesday morning
ready to begin her other life
in Larchmont, so far from Brooklyn
where she lives with friends
who know her from Ecuador, her home
where arroz con frijoles is eaten and Spanish spoken.

In this house only English is spoken.
Amelia requires silver polish this morning.
Where is it found in this home?
The Lady says, Did you ever in your life
see such a thing, my ungrateful friends,
I'm sure your people are kinder in Brooklyn.

Today as Amelia awoke in Brooklyn
she dreamed of words spoken
near Quito, where her two sons live with her friends.
Did they talk of her this morning
or are they too angry or busy with life
to remember her birthday, to want her home?

Amelia doesn't feel at home
in this house. At least in Brooklyn
she can talk freely of work and life
and loss when Spanish is spoken
as it was near Quito this morning.
Tonight she will call her sons and friends.

Feliz cumpleanos. Later she'll eat out with friends.
Me falta churrasco. She misses much from home,
like the clamor of her sons. This morning

she rose from her single bed in Brooklyn,
to the smell of coffee, few words spoken.
This wasn't what she expected, not this life.

She came to America for money and a new life
for her sons. Amelia will send a computer to her friends.
The Lady and she have never spoken
of why Amelia works seven days, is rarely home,
or why she travels so far from Brooklyn.
Yet, she is pleased by Amelia's smile this morning.

Back in Brooklyn, Amelia celebrates with friends.
They toast To Life! They chatter. What is unspoken

was said at home by two boys in Quito this morning.

The Day Before Thanksgiving, Erev Thanksgiving

Why will this Thanksgiving be different?

We will cook a small meal for one or a few.
We will gather with children, friends and family
    on Zoom, instead of our dining room.
We will be beset with longing,
    (while blessed with belonging),
    for the simple luxury of being together,
    in the same room at the same time,
    somehow,
    someday.
We will find a way,
Come what may.

News of the Day

After two, or is it three,
years of a liminal state
of being house bound
during those Pandemic
days that stretched into
months then years when
we put off doctors, weddings,
dinners with friends,
eating out, bowling, theatre,
almost anywhere indoors,
we nestled in our cozy place,
made a cocoon, got to know the
UPS and FedEx fellows
better than we ever thought
we could or would.

We got to know the dogs walking
   our neighbors,
our neighbors talking outside,
the night sky, the morning mist.

Zoom became a word that lost its
   meaning for what used to be
   a setting on digital cameras
   we no longer use or even own.

So – they say you sow what you reap.
And now, what we reap is desire, desire.
What we desire is real –
   real life, real people, real soon, really.

All the Ways to Say Thank You

It goes without saying,
that is to say,
I have to tell you,
in other words,
which is to say,
thank you so much.
I really appreciate it.
I am so grateful.
It was so kind of you
    to say
    to do
    to give
    to be...

May you be blessed
with all good things,
great and small.
May this be just the beginning –

that after the birdfeeder
broke, and fell onto the lush, thick
snow, the birds found the seeds
that had fallen from the birdfeeder,
to under the awning,
so the birds could still find them.

Thank you. You were here.
You lived. You mattered.

Comfort

Triggers That Make You Happy

What if a trigger isn't something that makes you
    want to scream and shout
    at the person or yourself?

What if a trigger makes you happy,
    if it makes you want to get up and dance,
    or laugh and jump for joy,
    or sing a song off key,
    or shout, Yay, at the top of your lungs?

What if the trigger is your own grandson
    reaching out to hug you
    or your daughter saying, Yes, Mom,
    you were a great mother?

What if the trigger is the bus driver
    this morning, giving you a big smile,
    warmly saying, simply, good morning?

What if the trigger is nothing at all,
    just you looking up at the sky
    tonight, with its crescent moon,
    its infinitude of stars,
    on this cold winter night,

and you know at that moment,
    right then, right there, that

Life isn't awful, after all.
Life is pretty awesome
    most of the time.

Life is full of awe, and that some
    awe is way better than none.

What Makes You Human

Truth be told, and don't be always telling it,
I don't really know
What this means, "I'm only human."

I've said it myself.

Is it a kind of shorthand for
"Well, we all make mistakes."

Then, there's the poet who asks
you to understand the "human truths"
of our experience.

What does that even mean?
Is he asking, "How are you feeling?

"How are you feeling?

So, you want to be happy.
You don't want to suffer.

As a baby, when you cried,
Someone changed your diaper.
When you laughed, someone laughed with you.

This much is true, this is all to say
that happiness exists right here,
right now.
Right?

Word of the Day: Saudade

I learned today that there's a word
    in Portugese for how I feel
    about Jennifer's grandmother's
    meatballs from when
    I was five years old.

I think about them often –
    surely, when I order
    spaghetti and meatballs
    at what I pray
    is a restaurant that knows
    how to make meatballs.

Her grandmother's meatballs
    were large, and smelled
    like heaven as they cooked
    all day in red sauce,
    her grandmother stirring
    with a wooden spoon
    again & and again & again.

They smelled like happiness,
    like how a full moon, or
    a rainbow, or
    your baby daughter's first
    smile would smell
    if you could eat it.

Your Birthday

For my grandson

It was a day like any other,
Except, for this, you were born.
Three days later, I walked into the room
Where you were sleeping, as newborns
do, most of the time.
For entering this world is no easy task,
And the tears started flowing.
Mine, not yours.
What I mean to say is this –
The tears were like a cup overflowing.
I knew, in those moments, that love
is the answer, that it is love that heals,
That it is love that makes the broken whole.

Reconciling with Happiness

All happy families are alike, each unhappy
family is unhappy in its own way.
~ Leo Tolstoy

Dear Mr. Tolstoy, if you mean to say that each happy
Person is alike, please forgive me, but I disagree.

A child once said that you shouldn't need a reason
To be happy, only a reason to be unhappy.

Ms. Dickinson longed for love, yet was happy
Wearing white in winter, writing neatly
On delicate paper, long into the night.

Monsieur Monet refused to work the grocery
Business, but how he loved his water lilies,
And the seasons changing with the light.

As a child, William Kirby played with bugs,
Studied English bees, and later
Spent his days and nights on entomology.

Mr. Newton disliked his stepfather, hated farming,
And lost himself building sundials, and models of windmills,
Among other mathematical and scientific things.

As I rise from my writing table, I bring my face real close
    To twelve daffodils in a blue vase – you can breathe in
    The sweetness of my Brooklyn garden from long ago.

Oleander

Imagine you're a pony
And you have to pretend
You're a giraffe, instead,
So that the other animals
Will like you, invite
You to tea, let you be buried,
When the time comes,
In their giraffe cemetery.

You stretch your neck,
As far as you can,
But it doesn't work.
So you form your own
Pony club, and hate
The giraffes for keeping
You out, and yourself
For keeping you in

A locked club where only pure
bred ponies are invited to join.

Any pony with a bit of giraffe
Blood is verboten (maybe a great
Great uncle fell in love
With a giraffe girl long ago).

Their cruelty eats at them.
The giraffes eat the light pink
And red oleander flowers,
You and your pony colleagues
Eat the yellow and dark pink poison.

Each morning begins with reading
And eating the bad news of the day.

Nevertheless, a still small voice tells you --
Something wonderful is about to happen.

A Gift

The rabbi said that forgiveness
is not for the person
you forgive; it is a gift
that you give to yourself.

It washes you clean
of all the hate, resentment
and anger, of all the ugly words
said to you, and that you said
in response, and that you said
to yourself in the aftermath.

It is the laundry aired
in the light of day, with the sun
shining on the line stretching
from your little house
to your little garage
that is never used because,
frankly, you don't own a car.

What you do own is a book,
many books, in fact, and they
almost always help you
to find your way to yourself –
    to forget.

Are forgetting and forgiving friends
holding hands by the sea, breathing
in the air of the next wave
and the honey glow of the perfect moon?

 48

Portal on the Queen Mary 2

Looking out the portal
Of this ship,
It's a slippery
Slope to prose
From poetry,
In the middle of this
Cold and stirring
Atlantic, an orange
Half moon above us.
Does the moon
Feel jealousy, or hope,
I wonder, for the sun
Whose red blaze, burning,
Startles at dawn?
Its extravagance of habit
Is not boring. It's Prozac,
Buttered warm toast
With a nice cup of tea,
A scone with clotted cream:
the world is all right.

What I see through
The portal changes,
And I change
Inside from prosody
To poetry.
Look! A thick morning
Sunlight where everything
Is possible.
By sunset, the possibilities,

Once endless, are one.

Pray with me, for a moment
Of grace, for the sun
In comforting routine,
In steadfastness.
In beauty it burns,
The day is not lost, it is won,
If only you are awake,
Awake to see it: Pay attention.

Shabbat

Shabbat is the pause button between
last week and next week.

Shabbat is the white space on the page:
it creates the letters, the words, the poem.

Shabbat is the cup from which you drink
the potable water of wells and lakes.

Shabbat is creation from which everything
and everyone springs, it is summer, fall,

and winter. Shabbat is where and when,
how and why I begin, and you end.

It is my beloved and me, we, in love,
and time with no beginning, no end.

The Olympic Spirit

No matter how low a person can stoop,
they can always stoop a little lower,
is a line I remember, more or less,
from Oliver Goldsmith's, She Stoops to Conquer,
a line that echoed in my ear,
since my own college days, every time
a person hurled insults, was rude to me, or a bank teller,
whenever people slowed to watch a car crash,
or the time in Whole Foods when a woman yelled
at an older woman in a wheelchair, maybe her mother,
for leaving the spot she was commanded to occupy.

But every time a world record is broken,
a spirit is healed and made whole.
What was impossible is now possible.
This month a French pole vaulter beat the world record
of 6.15 meters by one centimeter.
That's twenty feet and two and a half inches.
He jumped higher than a two story building.
Mark Spitz swam the 100 meters butterfly in 55.7 seconds,
and later beat his own world record five more times.
Michael Phelps did it in 49.82 seconds, beating his own
world record of 50.22 seconds.

Then I walked into Professor Smith's
class, and I watched him mesmerize a room
full of college students. He talked
of Clockwork Orange, of life, and Miss Jean Brodie.
Each student was given full respect, each student
was heard, and all of them gave him their love.

No one focused on the crutches, the noise outside,
or that he was the smallest adult human
they had ever seen.
Anything is possible. Anything.

Person of the Year

Outside it is raining, dark
   And cold, this 29th day of December.
As I write to you, Dear Reader,
   I sit in front of the fire
   And hope this poem finds you in good cheer.

I pray these words give you the courage
   To dream big, no matter how old you are.
In fact, I ask you to dream bigger
   If you are older – It will keep you young.

Maybe you want to help the girl in the next cubicle
   Who talks too much,
   Or the boy on the subway
   Who wants to sell you candy.

Or maybe you need the courage to begin again.

Do you dream of being Time Person of the Year?

Pope Francis was person of the year for 2013.
Pope John XXIII in 1962,
Martin Luther King in 1963,
Bill Clinton in 1992.

This looks like an honor.

Dwight Eisenhower in 1944,
Harry Truman in 1945,
Winston Churchill in 1949.

So far, so good.

FDR in 1932,

But Hitler got it in 1938,

And Stalin won it twice, in 1939 and 1942,

And there are still a few others with whom you

    Might not want to be on the same list.

Me, I prefer how they did it in lower school.

Each student got to be person of the week.

Everyone wrote him a letter, complete with

Doodles and drawings,

    That was kind of a Valentine.

You are good at art.

You are helpful.

You are great at math.

And so on.

Nachtmusik Sonnet

Even though I am old enough to forget
the name of my first grade teacher —
Have I blocked out the memory
of a school house, the antiseptic smell,
a concrete playground, metal swings and seesaws,
packets of two-cent seeds you bought in May,
five-cent containers of warm white milk?
Now I sit in this house with Mozart
and the sounds of traffic, a steady rain,
the feel of an impending storm
that tightens the stomach.
Still, there is something to be said for the music,
for the secret knowledge that the weather will change
and we will give a standing ovation to tomorrow.

Here I Am

Yes, you live in your body and your mind.
Yes, your home is everywhere,
        and nowhere,
        and always right
here.

If it's morning – begin anew.
If it's afternoon,
        no matter.
Now is the time.
As long as there is breath
        and consciousness,
anything
        and everything
is possible.

If these words find you,
and it is evening,
you, too, can begin
        anew.

A new world opens
        for you each moment
as you open a new world.

You're a Goddess

You listen. You hear.
You know it's not about you.
You listen before you talk.
You hear the subtext,
    you hear the heart talking.
You make people feel felt,
    understood, supported.
You bring roses to the conversation,
    and without a word,
        the fragrance in the air is sweet.

You're a goddess for these reasons,
    and not because of your charm
    or beauty (which you possess),
    not because
    you're married to a god
    nor because you live apart
    from other humans.

You're not a therapist,
    and definitely not the family dog.

You're just the next-door neighbor,
    the casual friend, the work buddy,
    whose mission in life
    is to bring peace and harmony
    to this earthly world

one person at a time.

Art

Not Enough

A poem needs to be about
Something. It's not enough
Just to feel something,
As you do when you listen
To Bach or smell good,
Rich coffee or see sunlight
Through the green leaves
of a maple tree
or feel Your Love's lips,
So warm, so moist.

Why Do You Sing?

You sing because you're happy.

You sing because you love sounds.

You sing because – why not?

You sing because you are transported.

You sing because you imagine.
You sing because something wonderful is about to happen.

You sing because you laugh.

You sing because it feels good.
You sing because life is good.
You sing because now is good.

You sing because you dream.

You sing because you love being on top
    of a mountain.

You sing because it's fun.

You sing because you want to.
You sing because your body wants to move.

You sing. You sing.
You sing out loud,
    loud enough for everyone to hear.

You are here. You are here.
You are here.

You are heard!

Safekeeping

I can't find the poem in the notebook
I put somewhere for safekeeping.
I can't find my passport.
I can't find the tickets for the trip
   for next week.
I can't find the coat I need now
   that it's fall.
I can't find the time to put together
   the book of poems
    I have already written.
I can't find the energy to organize
   the poems so I can put together
   the book of poems
    I promised you I'd publish.
I can't find the space to store
all the papers for safekeeping.
I can't keep all the papers.
I can't keep all the memories safe.
There are too many papers
   to keep safe.
There are too many memories
   to keep safe.
There is enough to keep safe
   for safekeeping
    if I discard something
I will still be safe.
I am safe.

Are You Ready to Write?

I'm ready – it's alright.

I've got a pen.
I've got paper.

The paper is lined and blank.

My head is full of clutter.
My heart is full with feelings

of Gratitude and Regret.

Regret smells like old broccoli or eggs left
    out too long.
Gratitude smells like a cup of cinnamon
    apple tea, or a plate of warm buttery biscuits.

To do list for today –
    Toss the eggs and broccoli.
    Enjoy the biscuits and tea.

A Poem Needs a Dog

to be a good poem.

People like to read poems about dogs.

They don't like poems about cats, so much.

Cats don't show you that kind

of unconditional love.

But you haven't met mine.

She lies on her back, begging

you to rub her belly.

Ok, you say, but she doesn't lick your face.

Honestly, I don't want my face licked.

Let her pretend to be a dog

and lie down on my lap

while I read your poem about a dog.

Settlement House

You settle in Seattle,
   unable to move anymore,
   done with your journey.
You settle for a little house,
   a little woman and little sense
   of who you are.
You settle down with all this
   like the baby you once were.

This is your settlement:
   final, everything is arranged,
   negotiated and discussed.
You're divorced from who you were,
   a life you once lived.

Really, nothing is permanent.
Isn't it true that in order to grow,
   you settle to the bottom to create
   truth and beauty, clear and quiet,
   orderly and decisive
   like winter on a summer's day?

Stilettos

Four inches! Good,
four and a half even better.
She held the satin
shoes in her hands
like jewels. Their straps,
so thin, a whisper
could detach them,
and when she put them on,
they were her brother's
red Corvette, her mother's double
strung pearls. She learned
to walk in them,
despite the pain, and
felt adored.

Peeling an Egg

at my kitchen sink,
looking out the window,
as I do each morning,
    I think -

What is there to say
    that hasn't been said?
What is there to write
    that hasn't been written?

"No one," you answer,
    but you, has seen
    this egg, this light,
    nor heard these birds
    this morning, only you.

You are the only one
    who can tell your story."

Citation

Previously published in an anthology edited by D.J. Moores, James O. Pawelski, et al:

Penn, Emily Lewis. "Nachtmusik Sonnet." On Human Flourishing: A Poetry Anthology, McFarland & Company, Jefferson, NC, 2015, pp. 166.

Aknowledgements

Shriya was much more than a Book Editor. She designed the website, and encouraged me tirelessly and brilliantly.

Catherine, whose beautiful illustrations, cover design and layout, gives the book life and energy.

Emily Lewis Penn was born and raised in Brooklyn, New York. She was the first person in her family to go to college, working her way through Princeton University as a tour guide in New York City. She also has an MFA in Poetry from Sarah Lawrence College. She raised her three children in Bronxville, New York and later, in Manhattan. Today she is a NYC real estate agent and poet.

Emilyspoetry.com
emilylppoetry@gmail.com

Made in the USA
Middletown, DE
19 August 2024

59451766R00042